Cécile Metzger

THE INVISIBLE BEAR

tundra

In a lonely, forgotten place, there lived a bear.
The bear felt invisible.

No one ever came to see him,
and he lived all alone in his colorless world.

Everything around him was gray and quiet.

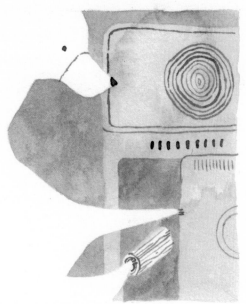

Then, one morning, a morning that began like any other . . .

Something changed.

Someone came to live next to the bear.

Her name was Madame Odette.

She lived in a cheerful world of color and sound.

The bear was not sure he liked that very much.

He was used to his peace and quiet.

But one day the bear heard something different.

My poor flowers . . .
the sun is drying
them up!

"Maybe I can help,"
the bear thought.

The days passed, and the bear and
Madame Odette grew very fond of each other. The bear
came to enjoy brightness and color, and Madame Odette
came to enjoy peace and quiet.

Then, one morning, a morning that began
like any other . . .

Madame Odette was gone.
She loved her dragonflies so much
that she flew away with them.

That same day, the bear found something
in front of his door.

It was a gift from Madame Odette.
The bear realized he was not invisible.
And his gray world would never be the same again.

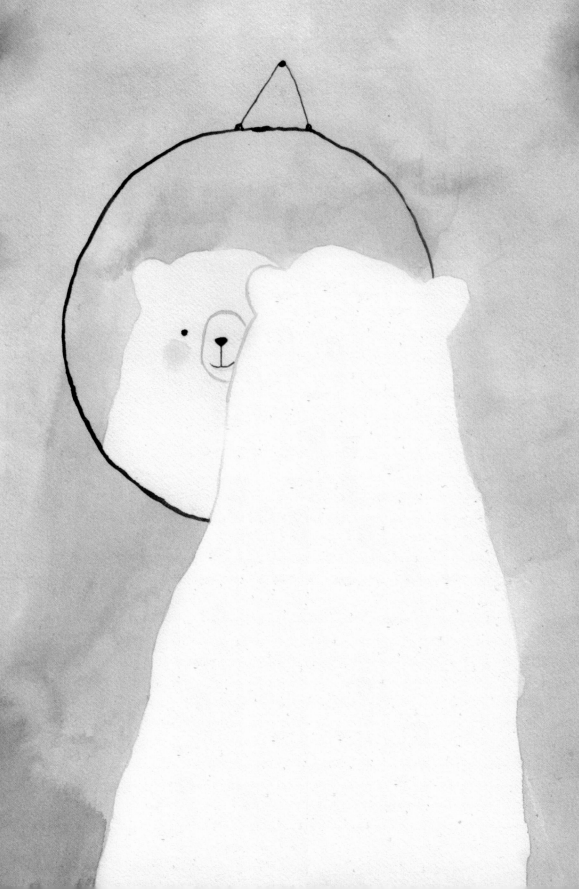

Tundra Books, an imprint of Penguin Random House Canada Young Readers, a Penguin Random House Company

Originally published in 2018 by Obriart Editions

Library and Archives Canada Cataloguing in Publication

Title: The invisible bear / Cécile Metzger.
Other titles: L'Ours transparent. English.
Names: Metzger, Cécile, 1996- author, illustrator.
Description: Translation of: L'ours transparent.
Identifiers: Canadiana (print) 20190146508 | Canadiana (ebook) 20190146524 | ISBN 9780735266872 (hardcover) | ISBN 9780735266889 (EPUB)
Classification: LCC PZ7.1.M47 In 2020 | DDC j843/.92—dc23

Published simultaneously in the United States of America by Tundra Books of Northern New York, an imprint of Penguin Random House Canada Young Readers, a Penguin Random House Company

Library of Congress Control Number 2019948075

English version edited by Samantha Swenson
Designed by Cyprienne Kemp and Leah Springate
The artwork in this book was rendered in Chinese ink and watercolors.
The text was set in Breathe Easy and Handsome Pro.

Printed and bound in China

www.penguinrandomhouse.ca

1 2 3 4 5   24 23 22 21 20

Penguin
Random House
TUNDRA BOOKS

I dedicate this book to all
the Mademoiselle (and Monsieur) Odettes
who fill my life with colors,
laughter and music.
—C.M.